CAROLINE PITCHER

THE GODS ARE WATCHING

Illustrated by Jim Eldridge

A & C Black • London

For Max

CHAPTER ONE

It's all the baboon's fault.

This city is a tangle of narrow streets, hot as a termites' nest. So I sit with my feet in the cool river and dream myself on to a ship with painted sails, blowing across the great green sea.

A voice shouts, 'Varro? Varro!' and that's the end of my dream. It's the captain of a riverboat. I've worked for him before. 'Unload this fruit fast, before it spoils in the heat' he says 'but wash first, Varro. You're filthy!'

So I have a quick dip in the river, and set to work. I unload the fruit fast while he's watching, slowly when he's not. Well, it's hot! The ripe fruit smells like honey. I fill my bag with figs, dates and sweet grapes. I'm paid for my work with food because I'm on my own, you see. I have no mother or father. I live by my wits in the city of the sun.

Some of this fruit is spoiled already because there's a foul, rotten smell.

I hear a grunt. That explains the smell. There's a baboon on board. It has glass eyes that stare at me without blinking. At first I think it's dead, but then it stands up on its sturdy back legs and hurls a red ball at me. It misses. The baboon is bigger than I am. It's a bull baboon, with a thick neck, scabby fur the colour of olives, and pink bits. It wears a flashy red collar with studs and it stinks. It throws a date. I'm not putting up with that! I lob the date back again, right in its face, so it hurls figs at me, faster and faster. I pick up a squashy ripe melon, but the Captain cries, 'No, Varro! Don't hurt the old baboon. My master says it is holy. It chatters at sunrise and sunset and my master says it is praying to Ra.'

The holy baboon puts its head on one side and looks at me. Its hooded eyes twinkle.

'It is my master's best worker,' says the Captain, cleaning his teeth with his knife. 'It picks fruit for him. That's why it's having a day out on the boat. Be kind to the poor baboon, Varro. It loves children like you.'

The baboon is not poor and I am not a child. I am twelve! The baboon grins at me in triumph. It lunges towards the amulet round my neck and tries to grab it but I push it away, hard. So it reaches down into the bilges of the boat where it has hidden its own little stash of dom-palm nuts. It crunches them noisily with big yellow teeth and looks at me, as if to say, 'Bet you wish you had some too.' I stick out my tongue. I never get days out, or my own supply of palm nuts. I'm too poor.

The Captain is talking to some boat builders now so I grab my bag and slip overboard. I need a break – away from that spoilt baboon and the noisy waterfront. I wander though the craftsmen's quarter to watch the weavers and potters busy in their workshops. Deep inside the goldsmith's workshop, firelight flickers on the treasures. Customers gaze at them with eyes full of longing. The one-eyed goldsmith is soldering two halves of gold together to make a bead while his son pumps the bellows with his foot. That son doesn't know how lucky he is! He's got a family and an apprenticeship, and he's never had to scratch a living on his own in this rat-ridden city.

Bam! Everything changes. My bag is ripped away from me! I struggle with the thief but *Ow!* I'm face down on the ground, tasting the harsh sand that blows in from the desert. There's a sweet smell of oil.

A voice full of venom hisses, 'Eat dust, urchin!'

CHAPTER TWO

I *am* eating dust! How can I help it? And I've only just had that wash. Now I'll be filthy again. I lie with the sun beating down on me like a hammer on metal.

I raise my head just in time to see someone running away down the alley. He wears a wig, thickly coiled and dark with oil. His curly-toed sandals – rich man's sandals – go flip-flap in the dust as he disappears round the corner.

And then there's a sharp kick on my leg. *Ow!*

'Which way did he go? Tell me, scum!'

This voice bawls like an ox. It isn't the voice full of venom that told me to eat dust. I raise my painful head and see the goldsmith, fists clenched, his one eye rolling with rage. He treads on my hand, hard, grinding my fingers into the ground, and then he puts his other foot on my head. I can see my old goatskin bag lying on the ground near me. Ripe fruit has rolled out of it all over the alley and burst. Ants rush from nowhere to gorge on the mess.

The goldsmith bawls, 'I could have sold half my shop to that customer! Anyone could see how rich he was! Now he's run away because you tried to rob him. Scum! Urchin! Vermin!'

Three names, three kicks, and he stomps back into his workshop.

I hope his fire singes all his hair off! It wasn't my fault. The man in the big oily wig pushed me down, not the other way round. He was trying to snatch my bag, I think, but I don't understand why.

I feel sick. I ache all over. My bruises will be purple and green as grapes. Suddenly I think of my sacred silver amulet and clap my hand to my throat! It's still there. Good. It is a scarab beetle, a token of Ra the sun god. It protects me from evil.

I struggle to my feet. I'd better get back to unloading that fruit. Back on the riverboat, I pick up a bunch of grapes but stop dead. There's a movement out of the corner of my eye, on the waterfront. Someone steps back into the shadows but not before I've caught sight of his big wig and curly-toed sandals; rich man's sandals. He's watching the riverboat.

It's the man who knocked me down and he's looking for me. Why?

I don't want to wait to find out. I crouch down and crawl to the other side, away from the waterfront.

Here comes a slow barge, sailing downstream. One, two, three—

JUMP!

CHAPTER THREE

When I dare to open my eyes again they look straight at stone. It's a huge stone obelisk. We have just had the Inundation, when the river floods and nourishes the land, so the barge can sail nearer to the temple to unload. I put out my palm flat against the cold stone. It feels wonderful!

The barge sits low in the water. Two small boats tow it behind them, so there's no one on the barge to give me away. I sit with my back against the obelisk. It's peaceful here, rocking on the swell of the green river and watching the water birds in the reeds. Out in the wheat-fields lie flowers and wine offered to the snake goddess, begging her to keep the harvest safe. The last few years have been terrible. Thousands of people have starved to death. But this year the river has renewed the rich black land and brought it life, and so everyone in Egypt will have enough to eat and drink, even me!

I'm thankful to lean against the cool stone because it is almost midday and the sun is full. Every day Ra sails his boat from one side of the sky to the other, carrying the sun. At night he sails out of sight, down into the dangerous underworld. Now he's reached the middle of the sky and it's growing hotter. I lie still, listening to the slow wing-beats of cranes in the sky above.

Then I hear something else. That's not wing-beats in the sky. It's the beating of oars in the water.

Swish! Swish! Swish! Swish!

A ship skims the river after me. It draws level. I can see the eye of Horus painted on its prow. Six crack oarsmen row this fine ship. On it stand soldiers in black, holding spears. And then I see him! He is jackal-faced, his hand shading his eyes as he searches the waters. I know who he is looking for.

So here I go again, vanishing, just like Ra disappearing into the underworld at night. I slip over the side, swim under the barge and stay down for as long as my lungs can stand, but at last I have to surface or I shall drown. There he is, still, bawling at the men in the little boats towing the barge.

'Have you seen an urchin with a filthy face? Needs his head shaving?'

They shake their heads, but instead of leaving, he turns to stare at my barge. He pats the coils of his wig. He doesn't know what to do. Then he raises his arm. His men drive their oars and the ship slices through the water towards me.

Take a deep breath and dive! I'm face to face with a surprised fat fish. Any other time I'd grab it but today's its lucky day. I stay under the barge until my lungs threaten to explode like rotten melons and I just have to get air, but I've got to come up on the other side from his ship, got to get my breath, whoosh!

They are still looking for me, so I gulp in as much air as I can and dive down again, eel-wriggling and paddling as fast as I can, deep into the thicket of reeds.

Stop. Tread water. Listen …
At last there's the sound I long to hear. It's the

beating of those oars going away from me, growing fainter and fainter. He has given up. He's taking his ship back downstream.

So I'll go upstream. In the midday heat the river is still busy. I know another boat will come along soon, and so it does, but I can't beg to travel, because it is a funeral barge carrying a corpse to the west bank for burial, with a shaven-headed priest standing in the middle of a cloud of incense.

Ah! Here's a boat full of goats with a peasant slumped in the middle. I call out, 'Excuse me, sir? Can I have a ride upstream? I'll work my passage.'

'Can you can milk goats, boy?' he shouts.

Milk goats? Anyone can milk goats! So I ride upstream with the peasant, towards his village high on a hilltop. We sail as near as we can, and drive the goats into some shade. With his crook, the peasant hooks down bits of leafy branch for them to eat.

'Get milking!' he grunts, shoving a leather pail at me. Who does he think he is?

Milking nanny goats is not as easy as I'd thought. They don't like me. They make foul smells and bleat as if I'm slaughtering them, and then I have to wrestle with a nanny who butts me in the face. I squirt out milk everywhere, on to my foot and into my face before at last I manage to aim it into the pail. The next goat I grapple with tries to eat my kilt.

'I suppose you lot are angry because my bag is made of goatskin!' I tell them. 'I suppose you think it was a friend of yours!'

That's when I realise that I haven't got my bag anymore. I must have left it on the barge. Still, it wasn't worth much and it was old.

At last the peasant grunts, 'That's enough.' He grudgingly pours me a small drink of milk and then stomps away to his village, the milk slopping in his pail. He might have invited me for a meal, but I suppose it would be smelly old goat stew. So I wait by the river.

It's late afternoon now and the heat is thick. Everyone is at home. I wish I had a home to go to. I wait on the riverbank for ages. I want to get as far upstream as I can, far away from that rich man who is hunting me.

Along comes a barge, full of stone from the quarries. I slip down into it. The barge drifts through the orange and brown land. A heron glides overhead to his home in the reeds. Ra's copper reflection shines in the water. He is just about to plunge beneath the western hills. I relax and sleep, long and deep.

When I wake, the world is dark. A great white lion crouches before me.

CHAPTER FOUR

I grab the amulet at my throat, begging, 'Protect me!' This isn't a dream. I've lived all my life in the city of Memphis but I've been told that lions roam the desert. In the moonlight, the white lion glimmers and the wind blows sand around paws as big as houses.

But the lion does not move. It has a man's face! I know what it is, it's the Sphinx, the lion with the face of a pharoah, King Khafra. It isn't a real live lion at all. Relief flows through me like the river flooding the hot land.

Over me, Nut, the sky goddess, arches her blue-black back. It is spangled with stars that sparkle like the sequins on a robe. Three dazzling pointed mountains rush up to the sky.

The pyramids! When our Pharaohs die they are buried in the pyramids. The Sphinx is protecting them, especially King Khafra. Their bodies are wrapped in bandages waiting for the return of their ka spirit. Once they have breathed in their ka again they go can on to their Afterlife among the constant stars. It's rebirth, just like the crops dying after harvest but coming to life again when the Nile floods next season.

Now the sky is turning pale like the inside of a shell. The pyramids gleam. Ra must be waking up and setting sail to bring us light and life and I can see that the desert is full of awesome presences. There's Sekhmet, the lioness of war; hawk-headed Horus and Sobek the crocodile god who guards souls on their way to paradise. The god statues are splendid in the dawn. I throw myself face down in the sand to show respect.

The gods are watching me! They frighten me, but they comfort me too. They will be here for ever while I scurry through this cruel world, looking over my shoulder for trouble.

And now there *is* trouble! Him. He's creeping across the sand on his curly-toed sandals, turning his head from side to side as if he were a cobra. Behind him slouch a couple of his soldiers. He must have spies everywhere.

There's a dark space in the gleaming wall next to me. I hurl myself into it and run, my footsteps echoing like drums, through a maze of narrow ways. It's a labyrinth. I race round the twists and turns and up a little staircase thinking, I wish I had time to read this graffiti scratched on the walls.I know I'm going back on myself. I know

I'll have to come out again right in front of him.

Ah! Here's another doorway. But it's blocked. It's a false doorway to confuse tomb raiders. There's an opening high up in the wall. I pull myself up by my arms and see a tiny tunnel with a sloping roof. I squeeze in and wriggle along as far as I can. It's hot and airless, I shall get stuck here and suffocate! This is what death must be like. Suddenly I know that this tunnel is not for people. It's for the ka of the dead in the tombs. It leads towards their Afterlife among the stars in the northern sky. But I don't want to be trapped for ever with the ghosts of strangers!

Something scratches my chest. My scarab amulet has come off its leather. I close my hand around it to keep it safe. I mustn't lose it, or evil can come straight for me, and I know he is down there, because I can hear him breathing. I can even smell the sweet oil from his wig. I tuck the scarab in the band of my kilt.

And then hands grasp the edge of the tunnel opening! I wriggle as far back as I can and hold my breath. The small hole of light at the end of the passageway is blotted out for a moment by his big, wigged head. I squeeze my eyes tight shut and wait, my heart jumping like a fish, until at last he hisses 'He's given me the slip. Back to the city!'

I wait as long as I can bear it, and then wriggle my way out to freedom.

'What are you doing here, boy?' growls a voice.

CHAPTER FIVE

A burly man stands before me with his arms folded and suspicion on his face. He thinks I'm a robber!

I take a deep breath and tell him, 'I had to hide because someone is chasing me. I jumped on a barge with an obelisk, and then a goat boat, and …'

'Who is chasing you?'

'I don't know. He has a fine ship and his own soldiers.'

'So he's rich and powerful. And you're not!' He grins. 'He'll be a lord or an official, high up the state pyramid. What happened?'

'He knocked me down outside the goldsmith's and grabbed my bag and then dropped it again, and now he's after me. I don't understand why.'

I know I'm gabbling. I want to cry, but I don't cry, because I can look after myself.

The burly man says softly, 'You're safe now.' I can feel tears welling in my eyes. This is what it must feel like to have a father, talking kindly to you. He says, 'These rich men are at each other's throats, all trying to get into favour with the Pharaoh. They're slippery as serpents. So take care. What's your name?'

'Varro.'

He hesitates for a moment. Then he puts his big hand on my shoulder and says, 'Come and have breakfast, Varro. But first you'd better wash. You're filthy!'

I'm tired too, but he gives me a bowl of water to wash myself, and it feels good. We walk to a table in the shade. He piles food into a dish and pushes it towards me. There is flat bread, barley porridge, milk sweetened with honey, and a large, cooked egg. I forget everything as I chomp away until my stomach feels it will burst.

'We eat well before we work,' he says. 'The statues must last for ever. Think of the Sphinx. It has been here for lifetimes, and the stone at the base is even older.'

In the cool workshop, half-finished gods stand around as if they are gossiping. There's Hathor, goddess of music and love and Maat, goddess of harmony, with her feather of truth. Jealous Seth, the bringer of storms and destruction, is carved in dark red stone.

'We've so many wonderful stones to choose from,' murmurs the sculptor. I stroke the mane of a lion carved from pale stone, and the scales of a greeny-bronze crocodile. The sculptor gives me a stone as cold and shiny-black as night. Basalt. It's beautiful! He finds me a little copper chisel and a strip of linen to wear across my nose and mouth to protect me from the dust. I hesitate, and then I start on the stone, and it's as if I've been doing it all my life.

'You have a real feeling for stone, Varro. What does your father do?'

'I don't know. I can't remember him, or my mother. An old woman looked after me.'

'Where is she?'

'She's buried deep in the desert.'

CHAPTER SIX

The woman who looked after me was called Pomfret. She was the nearest thing to a family I ever had. When I asked her about my father and mother she just told me they had disappeared. She said my father was a fine craftsman, but another time she said he was a sea sailor who gave me into her care when he left on a sea-going ship. She told me, 'Your mother played the lyre, Varro, and had a beautiful singing voice.'

Now old Pomfret is buried in a hole in the desert. I wrapped her in her best rug. I put in her favourite blue beads; a pot of hummus with a stopper of mud and a big jar of beer to keep her happy. I wailed and cried and piled dust on my head but I didn't shave my eyebrows because Pomfret always said that was a stupid thing to do.

I loved her. I think of her when I feel lonely. She was a wily woman who worked as a storyteller. She wore a cheap wig and had skin as brown as a date. She was nearly thirty.

Sometimes I still use her room to sleep. It's

small and baking hot, but it's safer than sleeping out on the street. Maybe I should go back there and hide? With a start, I remember Pomfret's ugly little house god, Bes, who watched over her. He was a grinning dwarf, made of wood.

'What did you ever do for me, Bes?' Pomfret used to shout at him, her face as red as a pomegranate. 'I have no husband, no children, no villa, and no tomb. When I'm die I shall be blown away like chaff on the wind!'

Bes is still in Pomfret's room back in Memphis, all alone.

'I'm sorry about the old woman, Varro,' says the sculptor.

I'm sorry too. Here at the pyramid settlement I see that they live and work – masons, sculptors, setters, carpenters, apprentices, and all their families too. It feels right. It reminds me how lonely I am.

'Can I stay here and work with you? Please? I'd work hard!' And I'd eat well.

'I wish I could say "yes", Varro. We have a lot of work, because the new Pharaoh is preparing his tomb. My wife and I have no children and I could teach you to cut stone. But it is the Pharaoh and his Overseer who appoint the workers, not me. I'm sorry.'

I stroke the black stone he gave me, and swallow hard, trying not to let him see that my eyes are full of tears again.

'The Pharaoh governs everything,' I say.

'He is our living god, Varro. May Pharaoh and the gods watch over us all. Otherwise chaos will sweep over Egypt.'

The rest of that day I spend watching the sculptor at work. He lets me use his mallets, axes and hammers and his oilstone for polishing. He shows me how to carve wood.

'Wood is good for practice, but it's very precious, Varro. Don't waste it!' he cries as I get a bit carried away.

He shows me a drawing on papyrus that he's made for a carving.

'I spent days getting the proportions right,' he tells me. 'That's the man who commissioned the carving. Look.'

In the drawing I see an elegant nobleman.

'He's handsome,' I say. 'Look at his fine profile.'

The sculptor chuckles. 'Varro, in real life he is three times as old and four times as fat. Art is not life, boy. I have to make him look perfect to flatter his vanity. And I had to carve his servants, his wine, and a goose too. At least I didn't have to flatter the goose! I want to finish that carving soon. Then I can begin my masterpiece.'

I follow his gaze. A hulk of bronze looms in the corner of the workshop. It has a presence as if it is alive. The sculptor strokes it, murmuring 'There is a sun god inside this bronze. I shall carve him and set him free so that he will watch over us.'

I need that god to watch over me! I had forgotten my troubles in this workshop. Now I remember my rich pursuer and his voice hissing with venom. I pray that the sun god will watch over me, and keep me safe.

The sun is setting, turning the pyramids amber and rose pink. They reach out across the desert with pointed shadow fingers. The eyes of the Sphinx become great black holes. I can still smell warm stone, even when the world is dark.

I don't want to leave here. I want to stay and learn to work with stone.

But what can I do? I'll have to find work on a boat, I suppose.

At dawn the next day, the sculptor pays an old ferryman to take me back. With a heavy heart I sit in the ferry and cup my hands round the piece of black stone. It's beautiful. As I stare at it, I begin to see the shape of a head inside it.

I can feel the eyes of the old ferryman on me. I take out my scarab amulet and tie it round my neck again. I need its magic to protect me. I want to fetch the little dwarf god, Bes, from Pomfret's room, too, and take him with me. Thinking of Bes and Pomfret makes me even sadder.

At last the white buildings of Memphis dazzle against the red land behind them. I thank the ferryman as politely as I can. His eyes follow me.

I hurry through the market, through a flock of geese that hiss and honk at me and trip me up so that I bump into a woman carrying a tray of bread on her head. Bread rolls fall everywhere and the geese stab at them with orange beaks.

'Filthy hyena!' snaps the woman.

I grovel around, picking up the bread but she's still cross, shouting at me and cursing that I am the lowest of the low.

I run on, scoffing the bread roll the woman did not miss, and stop dead on the corner of the alley.

Standing outside Pomfret's room are four soldiers in black. They are listening to an old man, chattering like a monkey. It's that ferryman. I have to get out of Memphis again. I'm still being followed. Why?

The soldiers burst into Pomfret's room and I can hear them smashing up her one small chair. A few seconds later, something comes flying out of the window and lands in the dust with a horrible cracking sound. I can hear them screaming with laughter, but the old ferryman croaks 'You shouldn't do that to a god. It's bad luck!' and scuttles away fast.

Soon the soldiers tramp off down the alley. I sneak out and pick up the broken god. Poor little Bes! His smile is spoiled and one wooden leg is smashed. The Pharaoh has hawk-headed Horus for his god, and the favour of many others. Pomfret only had Bes. But the ferryman was right. You shouldn't treat gods with disrespect, even if they are small and ugly.

I scoop up the bits of Bes and run down to the river, keeping in the shadows. I drop Bes into the Nile and he floats away downstream to a better world.

CHAPTER SEVEN

I have always dreamed of leaving the city on a ship with painted sails, travelling to Thebes, to Nubia and beyond to faraway lands. I could bring myrrh from the Land of Punt and make incense. I could bring back gold, ebony and ivory for the sculptor. Once I heard of a traveller bringing back a pygmy, a tiny man like Bes, and I've heard tales of huge donkeys with long legs … but I need to leave the city at once and the only boat setting out is small.

'Can I ride with you, please?' I whisper. 'I'll work my passage.'

The two men look at each other, then nod. So I drop into their boat and off we go. We are towing another little boat. But we only sail a short way before they steer into the reeds! They lift a big jar of barley beer down and stand it in the shallows to keep cool.

'Come on, boy!' they bawl and throw a tangled net at me. I unravel it and set the net to drift between the two boats. I have to wait for fish caught in the net. And the fishermen? They wade into the reeds and there they sit, slurping beer and singing bawdy songs about priestesses. I can smell the beer right over here. What can I do?

I'm stuck here now. I'll have to wait with them until they move on. The first fish flips in the net. I grab a knife and begin to gut it. I used to catch a lot of fish for old Pomfret and me. She loved fish. I wish the men would get going, because I keep thinking I can see the rich man with the oily wig hiding in the reeds. *Think of something else.* I lean back in the boat and trail my hand in the water and catch a lotus flower. Ra the sun god was born in a lotus flower in the waters at the beginning of the world. He made himself. He didn't have a mother or father, either.

The water is olive green and quite still. Pink flamingos stalk in the shallows. A kingfisher gleams like an arrow on its way upstream. An ungainly pelican flaps over, just missing my head. In the distance I see cows and sheep grazing contentedly.

A horn blasts and I sit up fast. There's a great commotion. A huge shiny blob is charging through the water. It's an island on the loose, an island of granite that rips through the nets. It rears up under the boat and throws it high into the air so that it smashes down in pieces. I strike out for the safety of the reeds and when I turn round the huge blob is rearing up with the second boat on its back! Its piggy eyes and the yellow gape of its mouth are right before me.

Smash! The second boat splinters. Water surges around me. The fishermen scream with anger because their jar has been overturned and all the beer has gone into the river so that the poor fish float belly-up, drunk.

The blob blunders around the river, blowing stinking steam from its nostrils. I don't want to wait around for it to trample me to death, or for a pair of angry drunks with broken boats to blame me for everything, because people always blame me, even when it's not my fault. So I swim away fast.

The grey-pink monster is heaving through the water and all the birds are leaving in terror. I hear their frantic wing beats. I'm in the middle of a sea-cow hunt! A boat sails straight at it, full of hunters poised to hurl their spears. The sea-cow bellows in fury and fear, splashing muddy water all over their fine linen kilts. Serve them right! Slaves are ready with ropes and knives, to drag it ashore, carve its ivory teeth, pull off its strong hide for shields and make a feast for hundreds.

I struggle into a lagoon and here's another ship moored. There's loud snoring. They'll have bad headaches, sleeping in this sun. Something glints in the sunlight. A harpoon is propped against the side. Its vicious bronze head winks at me.

And then I hear a *meow*. A small black cat is teetering at the edge of the reeds. I think he is supposed to be flushing out a duck, but he's frightened of the water. He'll never make a decent hunting cat. He's someone's pet. He's even got a gold earring. The cat is too terrified to move. His ears are flat back against his head because he has seen something awful hiding in the reeds. It looks like a knobbly branch, except that there are no trees here.

It's a crocodile. I can't take my eyes off that gnarled snout, flat yellow eye and the teeth that curl over its jaw, as twisted and sharp as hooks. A crocodile is always more patient than you think. It can wait for ever if it wants to, but this one has decided 'It's time!' It flicks its crested tail, slips into the water soundlessly and glides towards the cat, stealthy and swift as a spear.

Now behind the cat appears a girl. She reaches out for her cat. She has no idea the crocodile is there, but he's seen her all right.

You know me by now. I am not a brave hero. But what can a poor boy do?

I strike out across the water, pull myself up on to the boat and jump over the snoring hunters. I grab the winking harpoon. I steady myself, poised to aim, and all the time the crocodile slips nearer and nearer and *stab!*

Yes! The bronze tip is on target, hard, right into its spine. An excellent shot, though I say it myself! The crocodile twists and thrashes in its death throes, its red blood stringing in the green water. It is as big as four men. Well, maybe three. Triumphant, I grab the girl and her yowling cat, and pull them to safety. We collapse, gasping for breath.

But then I hear, 'Seize that boy! Don't let him get away!'

CHAPTER EIGHT

They stand all around me, knives out, as hostile as jackals around a grave.

'Shall we put him to death now, my lord Nebamun, or after dinner?' murmurs someone.

I can't believe my ears! But the girl runs up to this lord Nebamun and takes his hand. She cries, 'Father! You were all asleep, and the boy saved me from the horrible ugly crocodile. And he saved my cat too!' She turns to look at me with carbon-dark eyes.

Her father gazes down at her. How well fed he is! I have a strange feeling that I've seen him before … He wrinkles his nose, as if I'm a bad smell. Maybe I am.

'Father?' coos the girl 'Look how big the crocodile is. You can make lots of armour and helmets from it. Don't kill the boy today. He can be a servant! You said you needed more servants for your feast, and for Pharaoh's visit. Please?'

A syrupy smile oozes over Nebamun's face. He'll do anything his little girl asks.

'Very well, Kawit,' he says 'but first the urchin

must be bathed and shaved.'

Why does everyone want to wash me?

'I'm not sure I'm free to be your servant,' I say. 'Because I don't want to.' That gives them a shock.

'Stay with us,' beseeches the girl. 'You're such a brave and fearless youth!'

I put my head on one side as if I am considering their offer. What a stroke of luck!

'I'll be your servant, then,' I say and she claps her hands with joy. Just as I'm thinking she's sweet, she coos, 'Father, let's slit open the crocodile and see if it's got any peasants inside!'

Nebamun snaps his fingers. A servant draws his knife. He wades up to the croc where it floats, pale belly up, raises his arm and then plunges the dagger into its chest. He opens it with one long slash. Eugh!

'Oh,' says Kawit, in disappointment. 'Just a duck and a few old fish.'

Soon we set sail for Lord Nebamun's home, pulling the trophies of the hunt in the river behind us and in the early evening we arrive at a smart jetty.

I have never seen anywhere like their villa. It's big as a temple. The columns are carved with the lotus and papyrus of Egypt. There are wall hangings and painted floors and frescoes of birds and flowers. Everything is intricately decorated and very grand, but it's not very clean. Pomfret would have thrown up her hands in horror at the dirt. Everywhere is strewn with food, clothes, jewels and pets.

They have a sort of big bath outside. They jump in and swim as if they were in the real river. Around it grow acacia trees and plants to make it cool and shady as an oasis. There are lots of bathrooms and places to sit down when you need to (if you know what I mean). There are holes to sit on with bowls of sand underneath.

Nebamun has a place for his bottom only. He has a seat round it. It's a very big seat, made of stone.

I don't really want to be a servant, creeping around in soft kidskin sandals, being polite to Nebamun and his family as they loll around on the cool roof, thinking that they are at the very top of the state, and thinking that I am at the very bottom.

But I'm safe here. And the food is good.

CHAPTER NINE

Kawit twirls a sunshade of ostrich feathers round her head. Her eyes are ringed with black as soft as smoke and her hair is full of gold.

'The old Scribe is making papyrus out in the sun, Varro!' she sings. Kawit has persuaded her father to let her learn as her brothers did, but she wants me to attend her lessons because she says she's lonely. The picture writing is easy but there are seven hundred and something squiggles that the Scribe calls hieratic. We scratch away with reed pens and have to chant words and numbers.

The Scribe is as thin and colourless as his papyrus. He takes a while to sit down and cross his legs and every time he has to get up it takes him even longer to uncross them again. You can hear him creaking.

'Lady Kawit, attend, please,' he sighs, but she's heard the call of a golden oriole and is off out of sight trying to catch it. So he turns instead to me. His voice is sharp now.

'You seem quite bright for a servant, boy. You

could better yourself with the help of Thoth. Then you might even become a respected scribe like me.'

'I don't want to be a scribbly scribe,' I retort.

'So you aim to be a servant all your life?' he says.

'No. I'm going to be a sculptor.'

'Oh really!' he sneers. 'Do let me know when that happens, you cheeky urchin.'

I will, Mr Scribe, I will. And I'll be working on stone that lasts, not flimsy old papyrus.

Kawit dances back to us, singing, 'I don't want any school today, Mr Scribe.'

The Scribe shrugs, unfolds himself and creaks to his feet. He wanders off. Kawit always gets just what she wants. She has so many things, toys, spinning tops, leather balls and wooden dolls and animals with legs that move. She has boxes inlaid with gold and garnet and lapis lazuli, brimful of necklaces and beads, anklets and earrings. Her second favourite toy is an ivory cat that meows when you pull a lever. Her first favourite is the real cat with the earring that she calls Dearest. It hisses and scratches me whenever it sees me. To think I saved its life!

Nebamun adores his daughter and she thinks he is the very pinnacle of the pyramid.

'Father is almost as important as the Pharaoh himself,' she cries, her eyes shining. 'Soon he will be getting a top job as Grand Vizier. I may be given as one of Pharaoh's wives. Aren't you lucky to be a servant to such important people, Varro! Father is giving a feast soon, and we are going to see the Pharaoh make offerings around the temples. He's going to open some canals to imitate his great garden of Egypt.'

'You mean irrigate,' I sigh.

'All right, irrigate,' she snaps. 'And everyone important will make offerings to Pharaoh. My father has splendid gifts, better than anyone else's. He is having them made specially.' And then her eyes narrow like almonds. 'But he has a deadly rival.'

'Really?' I say, stifling a yawn. 'Who's that?'

'It's our neighbour. I can't bear to say his name because I hate him.'

Neighbour? I stand on tiptoe but I can't see another house anywhere. You don't get neighbours here like you do in the rat-run of the city.

Kawit cries, 'Father's gift will outshine all the others! Father will be Pharaoh's favourite!'

Her fat father is not my favourite. I have to hover behind him while he eats mountains of food and drinks rivers of wine, smacking his lips and burping. I have to wait with napkins and scented water. He wears gaudy rings on every finger and gets bits of his food stuck in them.

Then I have to clean him up as if he was a big fat baby.

That evening Nebamun is messier than ever.

'Varro,' he splutters through mouthfuls of salted fish 'I have something for you.' He reaches inside a box and hands me a fine copper dagger, as sharp as a serpent's bite.

'Take this to keep my Kawit safe!' he whispers.

I don't really want to accept a gift from him, but I can't refuse. And it might be useful if we meet another crocodile.

Later that night I sneak out into the courtyard and help myself to some sweet grapes.

Someone is talking softly out there! In the lamplight is a figure, hunched over a wooden doll. It's my master, Nebamun. He croons a spell while he sticks pins all over the doll's head and then spits hard on its face, swearing and cursing. He vows 'I'll have you hung up by your feet so that the birds peck your bones clean! You'll never live your afterlife in the field of reeds!'

I can't see the doll clearly, but I think it has a big head, or a big wig.

Lots of rich men wear big wigs, don't they?

CHAPTER TEN

This feast would feed the whole of Memphis. I count ten different kinds of bread and eight kinds of cake and Kawit says I must sample them to make sure they're safe for the guests to eat, mmmm! My favourite cake is the one made with cinnamon, cardamom, almonds and honey.

To prepare themselves for the feast, Nebamun's family wash in private bathrooms with their own special soap. They smear oil scented with lilies all over their bodies as if they were going to be cooked. I have to attend his large lordship's bath time – Eugh! – and today I have to administer his cure for baldness twice. It is a mixture of fats, fat from a snake, fat from a hippo, croc fat, cat fat, and I have to rub it all over his head. It feels and smells dreadful, and it doesn't even work. His head is smooth as an ostrich egg. Like all rich men he puts a wig on when he is in public, so why bother trying to grow hair?

The rest of him has to be completely hairless! He shaves his face and brows and plucks out every little hair he can see. He picks away at his rotten teeth with twigs and a kind of paste and chews herbs to sweeten his breath. It doesn't work. He still stinks of garlic and bad teeth. I moan about my master Nebamun, and Kawit's maid moans about her little mistress.

'Asses milk for her bath, and a mudpack for her face!' moans the maid. 'Who does the spoilt brat think she is? The Queen of Egypt?'

Kawit has green malachite on her eyelids and red stuff on her lips. The maid toils over her hair all day, plaiting and twisting and adding false pieces, and mutters to me 'The mirror is never out of her hand!'

Here they all have mirrors. Common people have to look in the river to see themselves, but even servants here can admire their faces in polished silver or bronze. I've never seen myself close-up before. I'm not bad looking!

We servants are sent to greet the guests. We have to bow and scrape and present them with flower garlands and cones of perfume-oil to drip on to their faces and cool them down. Some of them have brought their pets to the party. A woman with a shaved head has brought her pet goose. A man feeds a piece of ox to his huge dog. A young nobleman brings a sleek black panther on a lead. Who'll have to clean up after them? It'll be me, the youngest, newest servant, you'll see!

The guests lounge about on cushions. They greet each other politely, but sneak glances at each other afterwards, thinking Who's that? Who are they with? How important are they? How much did they give for that wig? There are no cheap palm fibre wigs here, I can tell you. It's all real human hair. They are so rich and privileged and full of self-importance. I'd rather be a stonemason making beautiful things. Instead I am just a servant boy.

'Let us entertain you!' cries the leader of a troupe of acrobats and away they go leaping, somersaulting and balancing on each other to make a pyramid.

A band of musicians bring lutes, flutes and lyres. I love music, I always have, and I listen to the lyre and think, my mother must have played like that!

A blind man twangs away on a harp while dancers whirl with their tambourines, singing to Hathor. They wear bracelets and anklets, make-up thick as the Nile mud, and very thin dresses. It's just as well the harpist can't see the girls he's playing for, or his face would be red as a radish. (I don't have time to watch them, because the bossy guests keep wanting me to fetch wine for their golden goblets, food for their golden plates.)

There is food everywhere, only the best and freshest. No maggots. Maggots are for the poor. The fruit makes my mouth water: velvety apricots and peaches, quince and sweet mango. There are bowls full of fresh berries, pomegranates and dates.

There's cheese, and there is beer, strained to get the lumps out. Oh, and there's wine, grape wine, ruby red rivers of it, plum wine too. There are salads of radish, lettuce, green peas and cucumber and the tables groan with piles of eels, pots of pigeon stew and a big wild boar with his tusks still sticking out.

I notice a duck stretching his long neck across a platter and remember plucking him yesterday.

There's beef, kidneys and honey-roast quail with tiny beaks. No goat. Only peasants eat goat.

The air is thick with oil burning to keep away the mosquitoes. Clouds of perfume waft from the melting cones of wax on the guests' heads. Some are inhaling mandrake root so that they can see visions. One whiff of the smoke makes me giddy.

Fat fingers snap as Nebamun summons me to his side. His face is already dripping with sweat and grease. He is dismantling a roast goose and squirting hot fat all over his arms and his tunic. Bits of gooseflesh are stuck under his rings. He taps his golden goblet. It is empty. Again! So I fill it with more wine and then fetch clean water for washing his podgy hands and rings. I want to get away from the thick, greasy smell, so I turn quickly – and trip up.

Ow! I've fallen over the lead of a jaguar. We're face to face and I don't know who is more horrified. Big whiskers, big cat eyes, big teeth ... Quickly I reach up to the table and grab a piece of meat for him. Big purr. Phew!

Just as I'm getting up my wrist is grabbed. Hard. 'Such fine clean hands on such an urchin' hisses a familiar voice. 'It will be a shame to cut them off!'

He is here.

CHAPTER ELEVEN

The rich man with the big oily wig who knocked me down outside the goldsmith's workshop and hunted me up and down the river Nile has come to this feast. Except tonight he is not in a big wig with oily coils. He wears a wig with long plaits instead.

What's he doing here? I thought this feast was to impress Nebamun's friends.

The grip on my wrist tightens. I feel sweat break out all over my body.

'Where is it?' he hisses.

'Where's what?' I whisper.

'The bag, of course!'

Bag? What bag? Then I remember. Someone tried to snatch my goatskin bag. He twists my wrist as if he will take off my whole hand and hisses 'I've wasted my time looking for you, vermin! Bring me the bag at once, or I will tell your master what a thief you are. You know what will happen to your fine hands then?'

Yes, I do. My hands hurt as I think what will happen, and my nose, and ears, because they may be cut off too. I yelp, because I'm scared stiff!

'What are you doing to Varro, my lord?' squeals a voice that must be obeyed. It's Kawit, acting like a queen.

He turns to her and says 'Little Lady Kawit! How lovely you look.' He's right. She has a jewelled diadem above her plaits and a beaded dress over white linen. Round her neck is a wreath of blue water lilies. He gazes at her, but does not relax his grip on my wrist.

'Father? *Father!*' she cries so that portly Nebamun gives a jump and shudders to his feet. He lurches across to us.

'What is the matter, my darling girl?' he slobbers, his voice thick with wine, and then stops dead.

'Minnedjem!' he says. All that wavery warmth has left his voice. 'Is there some problem with my new servant?'

Minnedjem. So that's his name. My master and this Minnedjem stare at each other. I can tell they hate each other by their tight smiles and dead fish eyes. I remember what the sculptor told me about noblemen. I wouldn't like to be one, even though they are so rich and powerful. These two would knife each other in the back just to get the last fig.

But my master Nebamun is going to put on a

show to impress everyone.

'Honoured guest!' he gushes. 'Respected neighbour Minnedjem! I trust everything is to your satisfaction? Does my feast please you?'

'Oh, indeed it does!' simpers Minnedjem, his eyes as hard as granite. 'I only pray that your offerings to the Pharaoh will be as impressive as your hospitality, lord Nebamun. My gifts for him are safe at my villa. I have an ebony box of delights for our God-King! It is a box as black as night, inlaid with ivory as white as the crescent moon.'

They are ignoring me for now, but he still has hold of my wrist. I can't escape.

My master's jowls are green with envy and his voice comes out in a jealous squeak. 'My gift is having the final perfect touches added by a master-craftsman. Pharaoh will wonder at its beauty. A top position, maybe that of Grand Vizier, will be mine!'

'Really?' sneers Minnedjem, twisting the fingers of his other hand in his long plaits. 'Are you quite sure?'

'Yes of course I'm sure!' splutters Nebamun. 'I told you all about it at the temple of the Setting Sun. You're so stupid you've forgotten, Donkey-with-a-wig!'

Ooops! A hush has fallen over the feast. There's just jingling from the anklets of the dancing girls. My master suddenly remembers he is supposed to be the well-mannered host. He grabs a dish of ripe figs and pushes them under Minnedjem's nose.

'Grown on my own trees and good for stubborn stomachs!' he cries.

Minnedjem shakes his head. I see his teeth and think of a hyena.

Kawit announces, 'We have the best servants here, lord Minnedjem, even if you insult our figs! Servant-boy Varro saved me from a horrible ugly crocodile with great big teeth. He saved pussycat Dearest too. Look!' She dives under the table and pulls out Dearest who is growling over a fish. He has an earring in the other ear now.

Minnedjem hisses 'If your new servant is so brave, then let me borrow him!'

I feel as if I shall swoon. I want to beg Kawit to keep me for ever as her personal slave, but I can't even speak, I'm so scared.

My master Nebamun cannot lose face or look mean at his very own banquet.

'I have so many servants. I shan't miss one' he says. He snatches my other arm so that I fear they'll pull me in half and whispers 'Go with him, Varro. Do what he asks. Spy on him and tell me everything he does. And don't let me down or, I will let my surgeon-scribe practice his scalpel skills on every bit of you!'

He won't get the chance because this will be the last time you'll ever see me. I don't know what Minnedjem wants from me, but I know he will kill me to get it.

And I still have to clean up the pet poo before I can sleep.

CHAPTER TWELVE

We leave the villa early next day. Minnedjem is carried high in a round-backed chair. He wears the big wig with the oily coils again and stares straight ahead. I have to trot along behind. Four of his soldiers in black march around me as if I am in a square.

But how could I ever run away? I'm too weak! I hardly slept a wink last night.

We board his ship at Nebamun's jetty. Minnedjem is carried under the canopy. He sends for me and snaps 'Where is it? The bag, where have you hidden it?'

'I haven't hidden it anywhere.'

'Then give it to me now!'

'I can't! I haven't got it. I last saw it in the alleyway when I was sprawled on the ground when I was knocked down by— by—'

'We searched the alley. The bag was not there,' he growls. 'Neither was it in your poky room. Where is the bag, boy?'

My heart thuds in my chest. I don't know! I'm

even too frightened to make up a story.

'I must have left it on the boat.'

'No,' he snarls. 'We checked both barges later, and we flogged the goat-herd.'

'Then – then it must be on the riverboat. The one that carried fruit.'

He slaps me on both cheeks so that my face stings, but I'm not going to cry in front of him.

'Then let us find this boat full of fruit,' he says.

And so we sail downstream, fast. His fine ship skims the water, seeming not to touch it. I hold my scarab for luck and pray, please, Ra, please! let us find that riverboat. I feel as if we will never, ever reach Memphis. But this ship is the swiftest I have ever known, and at last we are at the waterfront. What a relief! I'll speak to the Captain and get back that wretched goatskin bag. Then Minnedjem will leave me alone at last.

But the Captain frowns. 'Bag? What bag, Varro? I cleaned this boat from top to bottom the other day and I can tell you, there was no bag in it.'

The soldiers shuffle on the quay. One of them runs his fingertip along his curved sword so that a thin crescent of blood appears.

It comes to me in a flash. 'Where's the baboon?'

'He's at his master's orchards' says the

Captain. He glances at the soldiers and says 'I'll take you there, Varro, but I don't want to take them.'

'Lord Minnedjem,' I say, with a quake in my voice, 'this generous boatman will take me upstream to retrieve the bag.'

He sneers. 'I'm not falling for that! My soldiers will go with you and my ship will follow close behind. I will reward the Captain after you have returned that bag to me. Any attempt to double-cross me will make you much shorter.' He draws his hand across my throat as if he's cutting off my head.

We sail upstream. The Captain takes me to meet the orchard owner. The soldiers squat in the shade, sulking. I think they are sick of following me around.

I bow my head to the orchard owner and say, 'I wish to bid your baboon "good day". I had the pleasure of meeting him once and I would like to renew our acquaintance.'

'You mean Handsome?' He sniffs loudly. 'He is over there in the Beautiful House.'

A tear rolls down his cheek and plops to the ground.

CHAPTER THIRTEEN

The baboon lies on a table in the beautiful house. He is very, very still.

That is because he is dead.

'Hello, my young fellow' calls a man, waving a gleaming scalpel. 'Was he a friend of yours?'

'Er – yes.'

Fluid bubbles in a pot. There's the sombre black mask of the jackal god, Anubis. This smiling man is the Embalmer. He is going to embalm the baboon. Embalming was too good for Pomfret, too expensive for most of us, but the orchard owner wants his dear baboon to be with him in the Afterlife.

'If you'll excuse me, I'll just mash up his brain,' cries the Embalmer cheerily. He pokes up the baboon's nostril with a hook and scrapes around. He begins to scoop out the curdy white stuff that fills the baboon's skull. I cover my mouth but the Embalmer murmurs soothingly 'It's only a brain, dear boy. No one needs a brain in the afterlife. It will decay if I leave it in there. The heart is a different matter. We all need our heart!'

He exchanges the hook for a knife and in one sure swipe he cuts a great gash across the baboon's stomach.

'Good cut, what?' he chortles. 'I'll need to remove all the vital organs. See them?'

I can see that it's all dark red and glistening in there. I don't want to look any closer. The Embalmer hums a merry tune as he gropes around. He cries, 'Into the jars with dear Mr Baboon's bits! Lungs and liver and guts! I'll sprinkle him with salts to dry him up and when he's dry we can pop his heart back in.'

The Embalmer's eyes are shining and he sucks his lower lip in anticipation. He loves delving around in dead bodies. It takes all sorts to make a world. Or should that be, all salts.

Leaning against the wall is another baboon. It's younger and better looking than the old baboon was. It's made of brightly painted wood, not flea-bitten old mange. It's the baboon's coffin. The baboon will be wrapped in linen and put in this sarcophagus, along with his red ball and his red leather collar with the studs. They're waiting by the sarcophagus, but I don't see a goatskin bag anywhere.

Oh no! 'Are these all his treasures?' I ask.

'Yes. Except for fresh figs and dom-palm nuts for his journey to the Field of Reeds.'

The sight and the smell are making me feel sick. I stagger out into the sunlight. The orchard owner is sitting sadly on a stool under a tree. He says sadly 'Handsome was such a fine baboon, and such a wonderful dancer. I long to see him again.'

'He was a splendid fellow, sir,' I tell him, because I'm sorry for him.

'I think of my baboon each day,' sighed the man 'I picture him sitting up in his tree.'

I forget about feeling sick. Suddenly I'm listening carefully.

'Which tree would that be?' I ask, as innocent as you like.

'The fig tree over there.'

'Then I'd like to stand under it a little while, to pay him homage,' I say.

'Shall I come with you?'

'No, sir! It will make you sad. I will visit the tree alone as I leave.'

It's my last hope. I stare up into the branches of the fig tree. I don't know what I expect to see – the baboon sitting there, scratching himself, having a doze, waking up to fire figs at unsuspecting passers-by and then hiding?

Glancing over my shoulder, I shin up the trunk. Pooh! The baboon was here, all right. He made a nest on top of an old rug and it still smells of him. There are fruit skins and piles of date-stones and leaves. And underneath them is – my goatskin bag! I stifle my shout of triumph and put the bag over my shoulder. It's very, very heavy. But there's no time to look inside it now. Whatever is in this bag means trouble, and once Minnedjem gets his hands on it he will get rid of me.

Quick! I'm on the run again. I start to shin down the tree trunk.

Too late I see the upturned faces of the soldiers waiting to catch me.

CHAPTER FOURTEEN

We skim away on the swift ship. The Captain and his riverboat grow smaller and smaller behind us and I feel as if I haven't a friend in the whole world. I shiver as I wait for Minnedjem to summon me. But he doesn't. As soon as we reach his jetty, Minnedjem is carried into his villa, clutching his head.

Minnedjem is my portly master's nearest neighbour. They both have vast estates along the river, but they are different. Minnedjem's villa and grounds are immaculately tidy. There is no food lying around, no heaps of toys, no cat leavings or jaguar puddles, spilled make-up or pools of wine. Minnedjem is fussy. His villa gleams with polished tiles, painted with flying fish and octopuses.

There's the constant sound of shadufs supplying water for his bathrooms and filling the water garden. It is shaded with tamarisk trees and green date palms. Kingfishers dart hopelessly at the nets covering pools of golden carp.

The soldiers loll around in the water garden.

They decide to be off-duty and put their feet up on the carved stools. They even lift up the nets, grab a couple of carp, and start to gut them ready to cook. There's giggling and jangling at the gate. The dancers from my portly master's party are here! They make doe eyes and the soldiers sit up and stare. One soldier is sent off to ask for wine. Two servants appear with jars of wine and plates of honeyed dates, pull faces of disapproval, and then join in.

They forget all about me.

I've nothing to lose. I sneak off round a corner into another little courtyard and there I open my old goatskin bag carefully and peer inside. It glows! Light shines from lapis lazuli, rosy cornelian, deep garnet and ghostly pearl, all worked into a huge oval of beaten gold. This is gold for the Pharaoh! Only the Living God dare wear such splendour on his chest.

Minnedjem knocked me down, and hid this splendour in my bag. Why?

Because it's not his. He stole it from the goldsmith's workshop. Nebamun, my master, boasted about this gift for the Pharaoh at his feast. Earlier he had boasted about it to Minnedjem at the Temple of the Setting Sun. But Nebamun won't be giving it to Pharoah. He doesn't even know it's been stolen.

Think quickly! What will Minnedjem give to

Pharaoh? He boasted about a box of delights, an ebony box inlaid with ivory. It's somewhere in this villa.

And a black box with crescents of white is the first thing I see on the painted floor of the vast room! Minnedjem hasn't hidden it very well. It's asking to be found. I lift the lid, oh-so-slowly. It's very dark inside … there's something white down there.

Aaagh! I see the white needles of its fangs, its tongue flicking, hissing, hissing, and a yellow mouth gaping from a mass of coils that writhe and wriggle as it heaves itself out and flops on to the floor in a tangle of glistening black.

King Cobra!

It rears up in front of me, its orange hood flaring as stiff as a priest's headdress around its small face, and sways beguilingly. Don't look into its eyes! They are lidless, dark and glittering. They will steal your reflection and return your death.

The cobra is drooling venom. Now it's beginning to pull itself towards me, undulating across the floor in a dark wave of scales. I can't stop watching, as if it has cast a spell on me with its hard eyes. I didn't know cobras could be this enormous! It rears up again so that we're face to face. I can feel the air shimmer away from its flickering tongue.

It sways like a flower bud on a thick black stalk, then stops. Just in time I leap aside as it spits jets of venom that splash onto the shining tiles! Don't look into its eyes ... Cobras gaze their prey into a trance. The prey sees its death waiting in those eyes, and cannot move. Those eyes are full of my death and my feet have turned to metal. I'll be face down in the dust again, poisoned, strangled too!

I just do it. I stay alive. I snatch the dagger from my belt, sit on its neck, hard, and saw away, back and forth, forth and back. Its thick skin is crazed like cobblestones and cutting through its neck is hard work. Tough, cold and slippery! My arm aches, and I keep hearing the soldiers outside, they'll discover me, but at last the head plops off on to the tiled floor. A gush of dark blood follows. The body is still twitching and trying to wrap its coils into a ball.

All at once I start to shake. I realise what danger I've been in, because at the time, you don't think about it, do you? I thank Nebamun for giving me that copper dagger but I remember one of Pomfret's stories. If you kill a cobra, another will seek you out for revenge …

I stagger into a room and flop down on some cushions. A smiling maidservant appears with a jug of cool sherbet on a tray, and then disappears. I suppose she thinks I'm just another guest? She won't smile at me when she sees the snaky mess next door. All that black debris, blood and venom will take some cleaning up.

I swig the sherbet straight from the jug, and wonder why Minnedjem isn't hounding me for the bag. Then I remember my master, out in the darkness, sticking pins into the doll and muttering magic. Minnedjem is ill in his head! My master's spell worked.

In a corner, tucked away under a chair with carved lion's legs, I see another box. I'm over there in a flash and drag it out. This box is carved from fragrant cedar wood, inlaid with precious stones and on the top is carved 'To our God-King'.

This is the real gift. And inside?

I don't get a chance to look, because I catch sight of something moving outside in the courtyard, someone who knows they shouldn't be there.

It's a woman.

CHAPTER FIFTEEN

The fashion for noble ladies is to be thin. I realised that at Nebamun's feast. They don't eat a lot, but then they know there'll always be another meal. Not like me. I eat anything that Kawit leaves on her silver platter.

This lady is vast, like a river-cow. Her face is covered by her head cloth, and she has a big robe and cloak. How strange to wear so much! She must be sweltering. She waddles like a duck on big paddle feet but I can tell she is trying to move secretively. She's searching for something.

Ah! She's seen the black box. She stomps over to it and peers inside. It's empty now, of course. She gives a little jolt of surprise, and steps backwards, right on to the cobra's cold drooling head.

She sees the pile of twitching black coils and jumps up and down in disgust so that her headcloth falls back to reveal the bald head of my master, Nebamun! He staggers away, shrieking, 'Help me, Osiris, help me!' tripping over his skirts as he goes.

It's clear to me now. It was a trap. Minnedjem hid that cobra in the ebony box he described so elaborately to my master. He wanted my Master to find it. The cobra would kill Nebamun and then Minnedjem could present both gifts to the Pharaoh. He went to the goldsmith's workshop and stole Nebamun's gift. Unfortunately he was followed out by the goldsmith who thought he looked a promising customer. Minnedjem couldn't risk the shame of being discovered, so he dumped the jewels on me and planned to get them back later!

I was just in the wrong place at the wrong time, escaping that smelly old baboon.

I am in the middle. Me. A poor street boy, an orphan. I am caught between two rich, deadly rivals. I've got to get out of here, fast, and I'm taking the gifts with me, because I can bargain for my life with them! Luckily, the soldiers are drunk. They flirt with the dancers and swim in the carp ponds. One of them surfaces with a water lily on his head. Another is relieving himself against a tree.

So I help myself to bread, a lump of cold river-cow, and fill a gourd with drinking water. In the stables I find a white donkey. There's a silk cover for her back and a wide belt to strap on her panniers.

I sneak out of the courtyard, leading the

white donkey, praying she won't begin to bray. I touch my scarab amulet and look up at the sky. I ask Ra, 'Mighty God of the Sun, help me find the way.'

Just for a moment, I see three points on the face of the sun. They make two eyes and a mouth. Ra has heard me! His face dazzles me and makes me remember that the pyramids shine like mirrors.

It's a sign. I know where I must go.

CHAPTER SIXTEEN

I have ridden many donkeys, but never one like this! Most donkeys are dull brown and spend their lives carrying families, fruit and wine, until their poor backs are bowed and almost broken. But Minnedjem's she-donkey is white and pretty and carries me quickly north, towards Memphis, and on towards the pyramid; me and the gold in the bag and the cedar wood box. I'll call her Lily.

We trot along with me bumping up and down on her back. That night we rest in an oasis. I dine on succulent cold river-cow, and the dates and tomatoes are sweet. Maybe my luck has changed. I shall wait another day here, because I need to rest. I sit in the shade of an acacia tree and take out my stone. I carve happily all day until I've shaped a human head.

The next day Lily and I are rested and watered and it's time to brave the waterfront, but not as Varro and Lily, in case we are recognised. I take Lily's saddlecloth and wrap it over my head so that you can't see my face. I smear black river mud on Lily's white flanks. Now she won't stand out as a rich man's beast. She seems to like the cool mud being put on. It dries in a dark crust and I put some on my face, too.

We sneak into the shimmering city. I'm heading through the market and the craftsmen's workshops, towards the waterfront, hoping to find the riverboat Captain. There is no one else I can trust. He'll take us downstream, I'm sure.

Going past a beer stall I see an old crocodile snoring in the sun. The ferryman. I make the sign against the evil eye and hurry past, and then I have to edge Lily against the wall because some servants are jogging past carrying a big litter. They stop, sweating and panting, and set it down thankfully.

A plump hand appears round the ornate curtains. I recognise those rings. It is my master, Nebamun. He's not in lady's clothes today. I pull the cloth across my face but he doesn't even glance my way. He stomps towards the goldsmith's workshop.

'Oh! My lord Nebamun!' cries the goldsmith. 'I did not expect to see you so soon.'

'Pharaoh is making his visit earlier,' booms my master, 'so I shall collect my gift today.'

The colour drains from the goldsmith's face. His one eye blinks frantically.

'My lord, a terrible disaster befell us. We had a robbery. It was some time before we discovered that your gift was stolen. We think the robber may have been a vagabond boy. I have been working on a replacement ever since. See my blackened hands?'

He waves his discoloured hands before Nebamun's furious face. 'And I just can't get the right blue for the lapis, my lord.'

Nebamun clicks fat fingers. A servant hands him a stick. He begins to beat the poor goldsmith around the head.

That goldsmith believes I stole Pharaoh's jewellery. I see now that the riverboat Captain will not have been rewarded because I never returned the bag, so I can't rely on him. The old ferryman may wake and see me at any moment.

There's no one in this city I can trust! This is the worst place in the world for me today, so we will have to go overland. I feel as though I am trapped in a labyrinth built by the greedy lords. I can't find the way out. Every doorway is blocked. There's only one way out, only one way to escape. So I must take it.

So away we trot, out of the city and into the desert.

CHAPTER SEVENTEEN

Ahead of me stretches a golden eternity of sand under a turquoise sky.

A falcon circles above us. I wonder if this is a good sign from the gods. I tell myself it is, and try not to hear the hyenas howling far ahead. I hope we don't meet any lions, and Lily jumps as a little snake buries itself in the sand in front of her. She stops and brays loudly. She's nervous of the black vultures that circle in the sky and the lizards that scurry away from her feet.

I'm nervous of the sky now. It's no longer turquoise and clear. A dark yellow stain is spreading across from the horizon.

'Lily, I think bandits are chasing us,' I say. The desert is a home for nomads, men who wander its wastes for ever. Pomfret told me a story about nomads eating boys. If they find a boy and a donkey carrying rich treasures, we won't stand a chance.

The sun is beating down making my head spin. I shade my eyes and think the sun has changed. It's dark orange.

The stain is still spreading. Some land rises to the west. I can't see if it is rocks or a temple, but we'll head for it and hide from the robbers.

'Come on!' I shout, but it's getting harder and harder to run across the burning sand. Something makes me turn round. The sun has disappeared. The wind is howling, bowling a thick cloud of sand that is almost upon us.

'Hurry, Lily!' I cry and drag the braying animal as hard as I can towards shelter. The storm hounds us, tearing the skin on my legs and neck, and the sheet of sand wraps itself around me, whipping my eyes and mouth. Ahead through the blur I glimpse a dark opening, so I shut my eyes against the stinging sand, and stagger on towards it, pulling poor Lily.

At last we are inside the darkness, sheltered from the sandstorm that roars outside. Lily trembles and sweats with terror so I stroke her and her breathing slows down. Outside the wind still drives the sand across the desert, blotting our view, engulfing the world in terrible dark yellow.

'We would have died out there!' I tell Lily. She looks at me with eyes as dark as ebony. She's not a happy donkey, but at least now her skin is not being raked by flying sand. I'd better unload her so that she can rest. I take the bag and boxes from her panniers.

My eyes are getting used to the dark in the cave. There's an outcrop of rock. I can put the treasures there. I pick up the bag and slide it gently on to the rock, and lift the box, thinking, I shall put it down carefully so as not to scratch the fine wood.

I'm just about to let go when I see the scorpion. His tail is arched right over his purple back, but it's too late to pull my arm away from his deadly sting.

I fall. There is dust in my mouth again. I give myself up to pain and to darkness.

CHAPTER EIGHTEEN

Is this the Afterlife?

There's a donkey here just like Lily.

Light streams in and touches my face. I get to my feet, wobble, and sit down again until I have stopped shaking. I struggle to my feet again and walk to the light.

It is the clear sunlight of morning. Ra is setting out in his boat once more. The golden sands stretch smoothly before us as if they reach to eternity.

'Did we dream all those billows of sand, Lily?' I ask her. 'And was there a scorpion?' She brays softly and puts her gentle nose into my hand.

I go back inside, over to the rock, and gingerly raise one corner of the cedarwood box. Sure enough, there's a squashed purple mess on the bottom. My arm is swollen and bruised and I'm dizzy and I wish I had myrrh and crystallised honey to soothe the wound. But I'm alive, and I like it!

I gaze happily into the distance. Three pinpoints of light wink in the sun. I know what they are and I want to be there, so I load up Lily and off we go. I think we should keep to the desert but Lily heads for the green fields down by the river. I can't hold her back because she's desperate. She is parched with thirst.

At last she stops eating. On we go. The pyramids grow until they fill the sky and shine like mirrors. I can feel the heat from the stone. The great sides dazzle as if they are sheets of sheer amber. A low murmuring begins, as if bees are buzzing nearby. The murmur grows and grows until it is a roar, as if the whole sky is swarming, with voices and laughter and the sound of trumpets. Is the scorpion's poison giving me visions?

No! As we come out between the pyramids we find hundreds of people, waiting, talking excitedly and waving palm fronds. A splendid party is approaching, led by trumpeters who lift gazelle horns to their lips and blow a triumphant blast.

The crowds begin to chant 'Hail Pharaoh, High Priest of Egypt and the world! Shepherd of his people! Gardener of his land!'

Now I remember! The Pharaoh is making his grand tour. Kawit told me about it. The Pharaoh will inspect the canals and irrigation ditches, and make offerings at the temples of Osiris and Horus. If he fails to make offerings to the gods, calamity will befall Egypt.

Here he comes now, swaying high in a sedan carried by slaves.

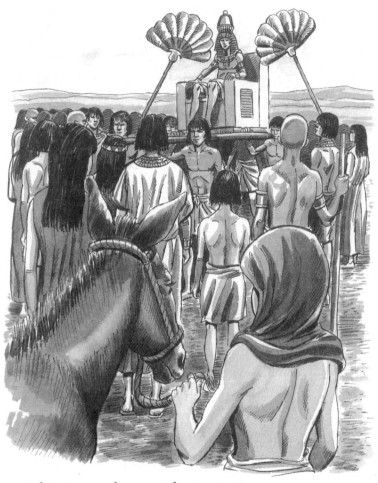

I have to take my chance.

I leap on to Lily, dig my heels hard into her sides, and ride straight at him. Everyone else is face down in worship now. The trumpets bellow again, Lily takes fright, trips and throws me hard on to the ground before Pharaoh.

Eat dust, urchin!

The dust tastes the same as it did outside the goldsmith's shop and in the scorpion's cave. Except that this time, the cold blade of an axe is resting on the back of my neck.

CHAPTER NINETEEN

'Leave him!' commands a voice. The axe blade is raised from my neck. The soldier steps back.

Old Pomfret taught me many things, including my manners. I touch my forehead to the ground three times. Then I look up at the great god-king of Egypt who has alighted from his sedan and is stifling a yawn.

Pharaoh's courtiers and governors scurry to stand near him, bowing and scraping. I know two of them. There is portly Nebamun in his pleated white kilt, and on the other side stands Minnedjem in the most outrageous wig yet, like a nest seething with asps.

The two men scowl at each other. They're like Seth and Osiris; Seth who chopped Osiris, his very own brother, into tiny pieces! Luckily for Osiris, his wife Isis gathered all the pieces together and Anubis embalmed them so Osiris could live again and become Lord of the Underworld. Nebamun and Minnedjem hate each other that much. I shudder as I remember that cobra in the box.

And they've seen me! So it's now or never, before they brand me as a thief and I get chopped down or strung up and never have a chance of paradise, here or in the Afterlife, so I've got to get in first!

'Great Egypt!' I cry 'I bring you something which is rightfully yours!'

Pharaoh looks quite interested now. I struggle with the saddle-baskets but in my hurry I fumble and drop the bag and everything tips out. There lies the golden pectoral, glowing with cornelian, lapis lazuli, garnet and pearl. The crowd gasps. (And they shouldn't really have their eyes open so near to great Pharaoh.)

'This I bring to you from lord Nebamun. And this, oh Pharaoh,' I stammer, struggling forward with the cedar-wood box 'is from his dear friend, Minnedjem.'

I sneak a look. Their lordly mouths are hanging open. What can they say? I am presenting their gifts for them, after all. They dare not let Pharaoh know that they tried to double-cross each other.

I ease open the lid of Minnedjem's box, fearing Pomfret's cobra revenge story, but the box is full of little figures. They are shabti for Pharaoh's tomb, to cater for his every need. There's a baker and a brewer, a barber with his razor, farmers and fishermen, cooks and musicians with lutes and tambourines, girl dancers with anklets that jingle, a scribe, a small private army with bows and quivers full of arrows, everyone and everything a god-king will need for his long journey to Paradise.

There is even a slave bearing a small mirror, and a stand of wigs for every occasion. Minnedjem has thought very carefully about what one would need in the Afterlife!

I like these shabti. I could play with them for hours (if no one was watching).

Suddenly I see gold filigree sandals. Pharaoh is standing right before me, Pharaoh, High Priest of Egypt, who has the power of life and death over us all. I can't help myself – I look up into his face. It is chalk-white with powder. He wears a tall double crown, red and white, with a vulture and a cobra with glittering garnet eyes and flaring hood, ready to spit fire at his enemies. I think, the baboon would snatch off your crown if he was here. He liked red ...

Great Pharaoh is not interested in the shabti or the jewelled pectoral either, even though it flashes like a kingfisher in the sunlight.

He says 'What's this?' He bends down to pick up my black stone. It must have fallen out of the bag along with everything else.

'This is fine work,' murmurs Pharaoh. 'Who is responsible for this?'

'I am, Great Egypt.'

'Mmmm. Not finished yet. But I look good in basalt, don't I?'

From either side of Pharaoh steps a lord, the deadly rivals, smiling at me as if they love me dearly.

'Keep the white donkey, Varro, she's yours' simpers Minnedjem, patting his asps-nest wig. 'I'm sorry I wasn't able to bid you farewell, but I had a headache.'

'Think nothing of it, my lord,' I say 'and remember to reward the river Captain. You promised that you would pay him when I returned the bag, and now I have!'

If looks could kill, I would be stretched out flat waiting for the vultures to tidy me up.

Portly Nebamun gushes 'Why not work for me again, Varro? That is, if Great Pharaoh would agree to you returning to my service?'

I turn quickly to the Pharaoh. 'Please, Great Egypt, I want to work at Giza.'

Pharaoh beckons to someone in his party. He passes him the black stone and murmurs 'What do you think of this work, Master Sculptor? Would you take him on?'

To my delight I see the burly figure of the man who was so kind to me.

'The boy shows great promise, Lord Pharaoh. I will happily train him,' he says. He steps forward, staring at me. He says, 'Varro, that amulet round your neck – have you always had it?'

'The scarab beetle? Yes. Pomfret said my father left it for me.'

He says, 'Let me see it.'

I untie the amulet from my neck and pass it to him. He stares at it. When he looks up I see that his eyes are full of tears and he tells me, 'My brother had a son, years ago. His wife died in childbirth. My brother disappeared, bewildered by sadness. He sailed to strange lands. Much later I heard he had died of swamp fever. We thought the baby must be dead too.

'That's why I feel I know his face. It must be like my father's. The sculptor is my uncle!

'This was his own heart-scarab, set in silver. I'd know it anywhere. And Varro,' his voice drops to a whisper as he glances at the black stone, 'it's not Pharaoh, is it?'

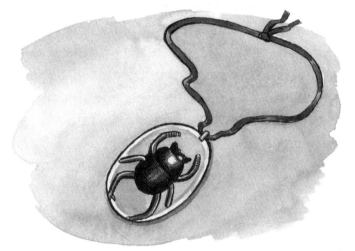

'No,' I say, 'it is going to be Pomfret, as she was when she was well. I want to remember her. She was so good to me.'

And the sculptor smiles and says, 'I don't suppose you recognised lord Nebamun as the slim handsome man in my drawing, did you?' and that makes me laugh out loud so that Pharaoh looks puzzled.

Trumpets sound again. Pharaoh calls to me. 'Go and learn from the Master Sculptor, boy. Who knows? One day I may commission you to carve me for eternity.'

He pushes the gold pectoral away with his toe and sighs. 'Gold is the flesh of the sun. Yet it is so commonplace. Silver is richer and rarer, I think. But stone is the true material of the gods. Stone lasts for ever!'

And Pharaoh strides back to his sedan, scattering shabti like dried bones in a game.

'Varro!' shrieks Kawit, skipping over to me. 'Where have you been? I didn't know you had that sweet donkey, or these lovely little dolls!' She puts her jewelled head on one side and her green eyes flash. 'You can carve a statue of me if you like, Varro!'

'I'll think about it,' I tell her. She claps her hands and kneels to play with the little wooden figures while I tie my father's heart scarab around my neck again.

It was gold for the Pharaoh, and silver for the street boy, but stone for ever.

ABOUT THE AUTHOR

Caroline Pitcher has always loved writing, and was encouraged by her mother and teachers as a child – although not by the famous writer, Enid Blyton, to whom her teacher sent some of Caroline's stories. Caroline says, 'Enid Blyton said the stories were all right but she didn't think I would go on writing when I was older.'

Caroline has since proved Enid Blyton wrong! Her first book, *Diamond*, won the Fidler Award for a first-time novelist in 1986. She has also won the Scholastic/*Independent* Story of the Year Award and an Arts Council prize. To date, she has published over twenty books for children of all ages, from pictures books to novels for teenagers. Her other titles for A & C Black are *Please Don't Eat My Sister!* in the Comix series and the Graffix title, *Cast Away*.

She lives with her husband and children in Derbyshire, and enjoys visiting schools to talk to children about her writing.

About *The Gods Are Watching*, Caroline Pitcher says ...

'I started reading about ancient Egypt as background to a novel for adults. It was going to be narrated by Cleopatra's handmaiden. I wanted to write about sun gods and baboons, scarab beetles and sandstorms, crocodiles, mummies, scandal and scorpions. I thought, Why are stories always about boy kings, pharoahs and other such celebrities? So I wrote *The Gods Are Watching* about Varro. Varro is an ancient Egyptian Jack-the-lad, a twelve-year-old filthy-faced survivor with no home and no family. Or is he?'

Another fantastic Black Cat ...

REBECCA LISLE
Planimal Magic

Joe is staying with his cousins in the
country where his uncle runs a scientific
research institute. Late at night there's a
terrible, heart-stopping wail coming from
outside. Who – or what – is making it?

When Joe, his psychic dog, Bingo,
and cousin, Molly, embark on a search,
they make a magical, mysterious
discovery which some people will do
anything to keep secret ...

Another fantastic Black Cat ...

JAN MARK
Eyes wide open

Six brilliantly-crafted short stories from
a master of the form.

Discover how the tooth fairy turned one
boy into a millionaire; how a reflection
in a department store mirror unlocked
a family's dark secret, and find out
how a misunderstood message
transforms two boys' journey on the
London Underground into a
comedy-adventure.

Another fantastic Black Cat ...

ELIZABETH ARNOLD
The Gold-Spectre

Everything about the wild Scottish
countryside seems unpredictable to
city boy Joe – even his new best
friend, Robbie. But the two boys must
trust each other when they try to
put right a crime from the distant
past, and face an angry ghost
protecting a hoard of stolen gold …

Another fantastic Black Cat ...

PHILIP WOODERSON
Arf and the Happy Campers

Arf is older and (a little) wiser and
ready to embark on his first hilarious
full-length adventure!

Arf expects to have to stay at home
during the school holidays while his
sisters enjoy a trip to France. However, the
plans go awry and he finds himself running
a camping ground and re-enacting
a battle between the Saxons
and the Normans!

Another fantastic Black Cat ...

SUE PURKISS
Spook School

What could be worse for a ghost than
not being spooky enough? That's
Spooker's problem as he faced his
all-important Practical Haunting exam.
It doesn't help that his task is to haunt
a brand-new house – hardly the kind
of dark, dingy place where ghosts
are meant to dwell!

But when Spooker makes a new friend,
he might just find a solution to
his problems …

Black Cats – collect them all!